BY JAKE MADDOX

TEXT BY
SCOTT WELVAERT

ILLUSTRATIONS BY
SEAN TIFFANY

STONE ARCH BOOKS
a capstone imprint

Jake Maddox books are published by Stone Arch Books
A Capstone Imprint
1710 Roe Crest Drive
North Mankato, Minnesota 56003
www.capstonepub.com

Library of Congress Cataloging-in-Publication Data
Maddox, Jake.
   Striker assist / by Jake Maddox; text by Scott Welvaert; illustrated by Sean Tiffany.
      p. cm. — (Jake Maddox sports story)
   Summary: Talented striker Jax Cooper has been Most Valuable Player for the
Screaming Hawks for four years in a row, but when he joins a traveling league he
finds out that he still has a lot to learn about teamwork.
   ISBN 978-1-4342-4011-8 (library binding) — ISBN 978-1-4342-4208-2 (pbk.)
   1. Soccer stories. 2. Teamwork (Sports)—Juvenile fiction. [1. Soccer—Fiction.
2. Teamwork (Sports)—Fiction.] I. Welvaert, Scott R. II. Tiffany, Sean, ill. III. Title.
PZ7.M25643Str 2012
   813.6—dc23   2011052569

Graphic Designer: Russell Griesmer
Production Specialist: Danielle Ceminsky

Photo Credits: Shutterstock 43565725 (Cover p. 64, 70, 71, 72), Shutterstock
82181065 (p. 2, 3, 68, 69), Shutterstock/Nicemonkey 71713762 (p. 3)

Printed in the United States of America in
Eau Claire, Wisconsin.
080317 010679R

TABLE OF CONTENTS

CHAPTER 1
THE CHAMPIONSHIP GAME

The crowd at the Centerville Recreational Soccer Fields roared. The Screaming Hawks were up by four in their battle against the Tigers. The winner of the game would be named the city league champion.

Hawks striker Jax Cooper watched as the ball soared into the Tigers' goal. Annoyed, he shook his head. "Hey, Danny!" Jax yelled. "That striker always burns you on that fake. Stick with him."

"Relax, Jax," Danny said. "Look at the score. The game is going fine."

"Fine isn't good enough," said Jax. "I want it to be going great — no, perfect. Come on, guys. Let's do that new play we practiced."

The rest of the team walked to the center of the field for the next kickoff. Rob, a midfielder, stuck by Jax. "I say we just do what we usually do," Rob said. "We'll kick the ball to you, and you'll score. We're all okay with that."

Yeah, I can score, Jax thought. *I just wish the rest of my team could.*

Jax jogged behind his teammates to the center of the field. The referee set the ball down for the kickoff. Jax bent his knees and readied himself for the kick.

Scott, another forward, kicked the ball to Joey. Joey nervously dribbled toward the nearest defender. In a panic, he kicked the ball down the field and into the air.

Jax ran through the defenders, watching the ball arc toward the corner. He headed back toward the goal. But before the defender could take control of the ball, Scott chipped it back to Jax.

With his heart racing in his chest, Jax kicked the ball as hard as he could. The goalkeeper leapt forward, but the ball bounced off his left hand and into the goal. Score!

* * *

Later, the team burst into Danny's backyard, singing "We Are the Champions." They hoisted Jax onto their shoulders.

He waved the Centerville Rec League Championship trophy in the sky. It was time to celebrate.

When the victory party was winding down, Coach Levinson cleared his throat and stood up. "Now, before everyone scatters, we need to select our spring season MVP," he said. He showed everyone the miniature trophy the MVP would win. Jax had three just like it sitting in his room.

"Jax!" everyone yelled.

"But you selected him last season, and the season before that, and —" Coach said.

"Jax!" they yelled.

"Seriously," the coach said. "Isn't there someone else who could be MVP this season?"

"Jax!" the boys repeated.

Jax sprang up from his chair and grabbed the miniature trophy from the coach. As his team chanted his name, Jax said, "It's an honor being MVP of the Screaming Hawks for the fourth season in a row. But I've got some news. As much as I enjoy being a Hawk, I'm joining the traveling league in the fall."

The cheering stopped. "Traveling league?" Danny asked. "But those kids are hard core. Soccer is the only thing they do. They never have any fun."

Jax looked at the trophy. "I know," he said. "It sounds perfect for a player like me."

CHAPTER 2
NEW SEASON, NEW TEAM

"Are you nervous?" Jax's father asked as they walked across the community center parking lot a few days later.

"Kind of," Jax admitted. "I don't think I know anybody in the league."

His father pulled open the door. "Well, I'm sure you'll make friends fast," he said.

The center was packed with parents and players, all standing around and talking to each other.

At the entrance, a woman held the sign-up sheet. She checked Jax's name off the list. "What position do you play?" she asked.

"Um, forward," Jax answered nervously.

"Do you have your entrance fee?" the other woman asked.

"Yes, we do," his father said, slipping a check out of his coat pocket.

The woman took the check and made another mark on the list. "Okay, Jax. You're on the Orange Crushers. They're over there," she said, pointing.

Jax and his father sat down on the bleachers next to a tall boy and his mom. The boy gave Jax a grin and reached out to shake hands. "Hey, man. I'm Thomas," he said.

Jax shook Thomas's hand. "I'm Jax," he said.

"What position do you play?" asked Thomas.

"I'm a striker," said Jax.

"Really? You must be pretty fast, then," Thomas said. "You need to be fast to be a striker. Like me. I'm the fastest striker in the league. So how good are you?"

"MVP of the Screaming Hawks four years in a row," Jax replied.

"That's awesome. I'm glad we're on the same team," said Thomas.

He seems like a good guy, Jax decided. *At least I know someone on the team.*

Just then, a man in a suit asked everyone to quiet down and take their seats.

"Welcome to Centerville Fall Traveling League," he said. "I'm Coach Jenkins. This league demands a serious commitment. It may be more demanding than what you're used to, but it's worth it. You'll learn the finer aspects of the sport, and our fund-raising campaign will teach you the hard work necessary to achieve goals."

Jax's dad raised his hand. "What kind of fund-raising?" he asked.

"The kids sell coupon books to help pay for traveling costs," Coach Jenkins explained.

Jax bit his lip. He didn't like selling things. "I don't know if I can do that," he whispered to his dad.

His dad smiled and said, "You heard the coach. This league is more demanding than your old one. But it will be worth it."

CHAPTER 3
THE ORANGE CRUSHERS

Jax stood next to Thomas at their first practice with the Orange Crushers. On each side of them were kids wearing cleats and shin guards. At the end of the line, he heard a loud boy cracking jokes.

The coach stood in front of the team and looked toward the loud boy. "Marcus," Coach said, "quit goofing around and listen." Then the coach walked down the line and handed each boy his uniform.

"I am Coach Marcelo," he said. "Here are your uniforms. Make sure you wash them before every game. I don't want your parents to do it. I want you to do it. Your parents are busy enough. If you don't know how, ask someone to teach you. If I hear that your mom or dad had to wash it, I'll sit you out for a game. I demand hard work and success."

This guy is serious business, thought Jax. *He's nothing like Coach Levinson.*

As Coach Marcelo handed each boy his uniform, he asked him for his name and position. Jax took his bright orange and black uniform and said, "I'm Jax, and I'm a striker."

"We have quite a few strikers on this team, but we'll see what you can do," said Coach. "Welcome to the Crushers."

Once all of the uniforms were handed out, Coach said, "Okay, boys. I want Thomas, Jax, James, and Marcus on offense. The rest of you take up positions on defense. Let's see what we have this year."

All the boys ran onto the field. Eleven of them took up defense, while Thomas, Jax, James, and Marcus ran to the middle of the field for the kickoff. Marcus looked at Jax and said, "You'd better be fast, man. That swoosh you see in the corner of your eye? That's me. Try to keep up."

Jax took the other end of the field so he could stay away from Marcus. He could already tell they weren't going to get along. Thomas and James took the inside forward positions.

Thomas kicked off and began a series of passes between Marcus and James. Jax ran down the field and found an opening. He waved his hands to get his teammates' attention, but they didn't pass the ball to him.

They each took short passes from each other and skillfully moved the ball down the field. Jax found a different place and waved his hands again. Still, no pass.

Jax was frustrated. *I could've scored by now,* he thought. *What's going on?*

Finally, Jax bolted through the defense. He headed toward James, who tried dribbling around a defender. With a quick move, Jax stepped in and swiped the ball away from him.

In a flash, Jax had advanced the ball to the goal box. Zigging and zagging, Jax overstepped the ball. He tapped it in with his back foot as the goalkeeper dove for his front foot.

"Goal!" Jax screamed, jumping up and down. But the others weren't celebrating. They stood and watched him. And they all looked pretty annoyed.

CHAPTER 4
TROUBLE ON THE FIELD

Coach Marcelo ran onto the field and took Jax aside. "What was that?" he asked.

"That was a pretty sweet goal, huh?" Jax said proudly.

"Yes," Coach said. "It was a fine goal. But you stole the ball from your own team to make it."

"As long as we scored the goal, what difference does it make?" Jax asked.

Coach Marcelo shook his head. "Soccer is a team sport," he said. "One person does not make a team. You have to rely on others, and they have to rely on you."

"They can rely on me to score," said Jax. That's all that matters."

Coach glared at him. "In this league, a team needs more than one star striker," Coach said. "The only way to win is by working together as a team. You need to learn to rely on your teammates. Don't hog the ball, and do not steal the ball from them."

Before Jax could respond, Marcus walked up to them. "What was that, man?" Marcus asked. "James was going to set me up for my bicycle kick."

A bicycle kick was one of the most impressive moves in soccer. If a player was skilled enough, he could flip backward and, at the top of the flip, kick the ball. Jax didn't believe that Marcus could do one. Very few players their age could.

"You can't do a bicycle kick," Jax told him. "I can't do one. In fact, I've never even seen one in person."

Marcus got right in Jax's face and said, "Then you obviously haven't seen me play yet."

"I'll believe it when I see it," Jax said, staring Marcus down. He'd had enough of Marcus's big head and his big mouth, too.

"Easy, boys," the coach said. "Let's finish practice the right way."

CHAPTER 5

CRUSHERS VS. CONDORS

Two weeks later, Jax watched from the sidelines as the Fighting Condors scored three goals in a row against the Crushers. The Crushers were losing their first game of the season, 3 to 1.

"They're getting killed out there," Jax told his coach. "I can score. Just put me in!"

"Sorry, Jax," Coach Marcelo said. "You're not ready to play with the team yet."

"Why not?" Jax asked.

Coach Marcelo sighed. "You're still struggling in practice," he said. "You don't seem to trust that your teammates will do what they're supposed to do."

"It's just that I know I can score," Jax explained. "Soccer is way easier when I just worry about myself. And right now, they can use all the help they can get."

"Trust me," Coach Marcelo said. "We're only two goals down. Their forwards are winded, and we've been holding back. Watch your teammates. See how they move together like clockwork, with a plan, with a goal in mind. That's what you need to learn."

Defeated, Jax sat in the grass on the sidelines and watched. James dribbled and lost the ball to a Condor midfielder.

The Condor quickly lost control of the ball, kicking it to the Crusher midfielders. One of the midfielders sent the ball over to Thomas, who dribbled three paces and passed the ball to Marcus.

Marcus broke free of his defender. He dashed across the midfield and split the Condor forwards. As the defense focused on Marcus, James broke away and ran to the corner.

With a well-timed kick, Marcus dropped the ball to James. Dribbling around a defender, James launched the ball for the goal.

The ball sailed wide, and Marcus stormed in. He flipped, and, in mid-air, kicked the ball into the net. It was a bicycle kick!

Jax stood up, amazed. As the Orange Crushers ran downfield for the kickoff, Marcus ran past Jax and said, "Did you see that? That's how a *real* soccer player does it."

Coach Marcelo leaned toward Jax. "James could have dribbled the ball in and scored," Coach explained, "but he saw his teammate breaking toward the goal. He placed that kick perfectly for Marcus's goal."

"If James had kicked it in instead," Jax said, "the score would have been the same. What difference does it make?"

"For one thing, that wasn't the play that was called," said Coach. "For another thing, I want my players to think of assists as being as important as goals."

Coach looked Jax in the eye. "A team full of boys that can truly work together will outplay a couple of goal-hungry scorers anytime," he said. "Now go in and give Vince a break."

Jax ran onto the field. The Crushers took defense and prepared for the Condors' kickoff. "Let's switch to a zone defense, boys," Thomas said. "We'll save some energy."

The Condors kicked off and strode down the field. Jax broke off his zone coverage to steal the ball. Before the other Crushers knew it, he had bolted downfield.

Weaving between forwards and midfielders, Jax never looked back for his teammates. Suddenly, he realized he was in trouble. His teammates hadn't reacted quickly enough for his break.

Now six different Condors covered him. He fell down, and they quickly took the ball into Crusher territory.

Jax ran as fast as he could, but he couldn't get back on defense fast enough. He watched James and Thomas switch off covering two Condors. But their quick defensive moves were no use. With Jax out of position, the Condors quickly scored.

As the Condors ran past, Thomas came up to Jax. "Thanks a lot," he said. "It only takes one person to score, but it also only takes one person to break the plan and make it fall apart. Guess we know which person you are."

"Dude," James said, running over. "Thomas is right, man. Stick to the game plan. You have some skills on the field, but they're a complete waste if you keep playing like that."

Before Jax could respond, Coach Marcelo shouted, "Get back here, Jax." Vince ran back in to the game, and Jax's chance to prove himself was over.

CHAPTER 6
BATTLING THE BOBCATS

Two more weeks passed, and Jax still couldn't convince Coach Marcelo he knew his way around the soccer field. As the Crushers took on the Bobcats, Jax sat watching on the sidelines.

So far his plan to join the traveling league was backfiring. Coach wouldn't even put him in the game, and Jax couldn't understand why. He felt like his skills were being overlooked. Why have a great scorer sitting on the sidelines all the time?

On the field, Thomas and Marcus led the Crushers to a 6-to-1 lead. *Maybe the team just doesn't need me,* thought Jax. *I should have stuck with the Hawks. At least there I was a star.*

Coach Marcelo walked over, interrupting Jax's thoughts. "Wake up, Jax!" Coach said. "Come on. I need you to give Thomas a breather."

Oh, great, thought Jax. *Garbage time. Coaches only put losers in when it's a blowout.* Still, Jax jogged to the sideline and bent into the circle to hear the coach's play.

"Marcus," the coach said, "can you take the lead on the field?"

"Sure can," Marcus said.

"Good," Coach Marcelo said. "Let's try that thunderbird offense we practiced this week. Jax, I need you to set up Marcus. I need a good pass, okay? Can I get a good assist from you, striker?"

Jax nodded and said, "Yeah, sure."

"Not 'yeah, sure,' Jax," Coach said. "I need a 'you got it, Coach.' Okay?"

"You got it, Coach," Jax replied.

"Good," Coach said. "Let's get it done."

Jax and Marcus led the Crushers back on the field for the kickoff. Everyone took their positions. As Jax passed by, Marcus said, "Stick to the play, okay? Don't mess this up."

Jax nodded and took up his position as a forward.

Marcus kicked off with a pass to James, but James lost the ball and the Bobcats dribbled it down the field.

One of the Crusher midfielders was able to get in front of the ball, taking control of it. He spotted James and passed him the ball.

"Great job, boys," Coach Marcelo shouted.

James dribbled up the field and made eye contact with Jax. As they headed through the defense, James passed to Jax. This was it. Marcus broke off down the opposite sideline.

"Stick to the play," Jax told himself. But as he dribbled down toward the goal box, he noticed an extra defender covering Marcus.

It would be really tough to make the pass. When the blocker in front of Jax turned the other way to check on his goalkeeper, Jax made a move.

Instead of passing to Marcus, he faked the pass and dribbled to the goal. Before the defender could recover, Jax blasted a kick. The ball sailed over the head of the goalkeeper and into the net.

Jax jumped up and pumped his fist in celebration. But Marcus ran over looking angry. "Do you call that sticking to the play?" he asked.

"They pulled an extra defender to you," Jax said. "I had to change the play or we would have turned the ball over."

Marcus shook his head and said, "I was going to split them."

Jax laughed. "It didn't look like it," he said.

Marcus crossed his arms. "Just listen to the coach," he said. "You're useless unless you're following the plan."

"I tried that," Jax said.

They kept yelling, both getting louder and louder, until Coach Marcelo came over and broke it up.

"Game over," he said.

CHAPTER 7
TEAMWORK

A week after their fight during the Bobcats game, Jax and Marcus were assigned to sell coupon books together for the team. They walked through a quiet neighborhood, barely speaking to each other.

Coach Marcelo had made them partners so they could learn about teamwork. Jax wished they could split up, but if Coach found out, they would both be in big trouble. They were in enough trouble already.

Dressed in clean white shirts and ties, both boys looked awkward and nervous. They walked up the sidewalk to a big white house. Marcus stood next to Jax on the steps of the house.

"Are you going to knock on the door or what?" Marcus asked.

"I knocked on the last one," Jax said.

"So?" Marcus said.

Jax rolled his eyes. "So you knock," he said.

"Coach put us together on the fundraiser so we'd learn how to get along," Marcus said. "So just knock."

Just then, the front door of the house opened and a woman stepped out. "Can I help you, boys?" she asked.

Jax held out a coupon book and said, "We're raising money for the Orange Crushers, our traveling soccer team. We're selling coupon books for ten dollars. It has over fifty dollars in savings at places like Nails'R'Us, Burger Town, and The Ice Cream Shop."

"I don't have time for this," the woman said and turned around to go back inside.

Marcus slapped Jax's shoulder and said, "Plus, we'll mow your lawn for free."

"We will?" asked Jax. Marcus nodded.

The woman turned around. "For free, huh?" she said. "All right."

Jax smiled at Marcus as the woman went inside to get her purse. "Nice," Jax said.

"I figure they don't want our stupid coupons," Marcus said. "But if we offer a little help, they'll help us back."

Ten minutes later, Jax was pushing a noisy lawn mower in the backyard of the big white house. He had sweated through his nice white shirt. In the next-door neighbor's lawn, Marcus pushed another mower.

Later that afternoon, Marcus and Jax raked leaves in a lawn down the street. One boy raked while the other held the trash bag.

Two houses down, they both clipped a hedge for another neighbor. At another house, they stacked firewood.

All through the neighborhood, the two boys worked hard helping their neighbors — and they sold a coupon book at each house.

After they were finished, both boys were tired, dirty, and hungry. "I'm starving," said Jax. "You want to come over to my house for pizza or something?"

Marcus grinned. "Sure," he said. "Hey, it looks like Coach knew what he was doing. We just might end up being friends."

"Dude, it's only pizza," said Jax, laughing. "Let's not get carried away."

* * *

At the soccer fields a week later, Coach Marcelo called his team together. "Two more wins and we're in the playoffs, boys," he said. "And thanks to our fund-raising leaders, Jax and Marcus, we have the money we need to make the trip to Springfield. It's nice to see that my plan worked. So, did you boys learn a little bit about teamwork?"

Marcus slugged Jax in the shoulder lightly. "Yes," Marcus said, "and we learned that our neighbors have really big lawns," he said.

"And overgrown hedges," added Jax.

Coach looked confused, but then he shrugged. "Good, good," he said. "Now, the Hornets are tough. They have a couple of the best strikers in the league. So I want to try something different. Jax and Marcus, I need you to work together again as teammates. Jax, I'm going to need to see some assists."

"No problem," said Jax.

"Piece of cake," added Marcus.

CHAPTER 8

CRUSHERS VS. BULLFROGS

It *was* a piece of cake. The Crushers beat the Hornets, 4 to 2. Not only had Jax made some great assists, he'd also scored one of the goals. But a week later, they had to play the Bullfrogs. Before the game, Coach Marcelo gathered the group in the locker room.

"Okay guys," Coach Marcelo said. "This is a big game. If we beat the Bullfrogs, we'll make the playoffs."

Coach pointed to Jax and Marcus. "We beat the Green Hornets last week because of Jax and Marcus's teamwork," he said. "They'll be looking for that again. So we have to switch it up. Marcus, are you wearing your goal-scoring shoes?"

"Of course," Marcus said. "Plus I'm wearing unstoppable defensive socks."

"Nobody would want to get near your socks," Jax said, laughing.

"No kidding," Marcus said. "That's why they're defensive."

The Crushers laughed nervously. "All right," the coach said. "Thomas, I need you to take point out there, be my eyes and ears."

"No problem, Coach!" said Thomas.

"James, we're going to need you most during transitions," Coach said. "Don't be afraid to get in there and mess things up."

"Will do, Coach," said James.

"And Jax," the coach said. "Use what you've learned over the past weeks and apply it to the game."

Jax raised his head and smiled. "I'm ready," he said.

"Excellent," Coach said. "Okay, alpha team, get out there for the kickoff."

As the Bullfrogs kicked off the game, Jax dropped into defense. Soon, he saw a Bullfrog mishandle the ball. Jax snuck in and stole it.

Most of the Bullfrogs were still moving from offense to defense. Jax saw an opening for a goal down the field.

But instead of dribbling down the field himself, he passed the ball to James, who had an easier shot at making it since he was closer. It went against Jax's instincts, but he did it anyway. This wasn't about him. It was about the team.

A few minutes later, he watched Thomas score the first goal of the game. Jax cheered with the rest of the Crushers. The beta team swapped out to give them a rest.

As Jax sat on the sideline and drank water, he saw Vince lose the ball to a Bullfrog. The Bullfrog player immediately sprinted down the field and scored quickly. "Come on, Crushers," Jax whispered.

On the kick-off, Daryl, a Crusher defender, blocked a clearing shot and passed it down the field. But a Bullfrog stepped in and intercepted the pass.

In the Crusher goal box, the ball got knocked around by defenders and forwards six different times. In the quick battle for the ball, a wide shot rolled past the Crusher goalkeeper.

Coach shouted, "Alpha team, get in there for that next kickoff."

Jax walked past Marcus on the way to the field. Marcus said, "Jax, T-bird-10. Get open. I'll pass it to you."

"But that's a play for Thomas," Jax said.

"Not this time," Marcus said. "This time it's for you."

Jax looked down the line at Thomas, who was giving him the thumbs up. "All right," Jax said. "I'll get open."

At the kickoff, Jax got into position. Marcus passed to James, who looped the ball to Thomas.

Quickly, Thomas passed the ball to Jax. But he was double covered, and the Bullfrogs gained control of the ball.

Frustrated, Jax fell back on defense. Marcus passed him and said, "Shrug it off. Sometimes the play isn't there. Work with it."

On defense, Daryl got the ball and cleared it to the other side. Jax ran down the field. He was wide open when he noticed that Thomas was struggling through the defense and needed help. Jax snuck up behind the defenders and got in their way to clear Thomas. While Jax mixed it up with the defense, Thomas passed to James, who put the goal in.

"Now that's teamwork," shouted Coach. "Tie game."

CHAPTER 9
A BIG FINISH

"Okay, boys," Coach Marcelo said as the players gathered around him. "We're hanging in there. All we have to do is stick to our game and we have a chance."

"What's our play after the kick-off?" Thomas asked.

"Let's start off in jaguar defense and see how the game goes," Coach Marcelo said. "Reserve players, get out there to start the half. I want to keep the starters fresh."

The back-up players ran onto the field. Jax rubbed his head with a towel. Then he sat back and watched the game.

Back and forth, the ball was cleared and cleared again. Vince broke out once and was about to score, but a blocker came in to break it up.

"Vince almost had it," Marcus said, standing on his tiptoes.

Then the Bullfrogs made a run. The Crusher defenders had trouble keeping up with the passes. Daryl cleared it once, only to have the Bullfrogs push right back down to the Crushers' goal box.

The Bullfrogs' striker set up the ball and kicked. The Crushers' goalkeeper jumped up and got a finger on the ball. The ball sailed high, bounced off the top bar, and went out of bounds.

"That was close," Thomas said. "I've never seen Ben jump so high."

"All right, alpha team," Coach said. "Get in there. Give those guys a break."

Jax, James, Thomas, and Marcus ran onto the field. They high-fived their teammates and took their positions.

"Stick to jaguar defense," Thomas said. "Keep it simple and safe. We'll strike if we get a shot."

Marcus took the ball and in-bounded it with a pass to James. They moved it down the field with ease until they got into the goal box. Then the Bullfrogs swarmed and kicked it out. Control of the ball went back and forth, each team keeping it clear of the goal. The game was exciting, but nerve-racking.

With three minutes left, Jax spotted
a Bullfrog trying to clear the ball out of
the goal box. Giving one last-ditch effort,
Jax ran to the ball and got in front of it.
It bounced off his hip and skirted to the
sideline. With sweat pouring down his
forehead, he turned the ball around and
looked at his teammates.

James took position across the other
side of the goal box. Marcus and Thomas
made their way down the middle. Jax's first
instinct was to try to score right away, but
he knew it would be too risky. He had to
trust his teammates to get free.

Jax reared back and kicked the ball
across the goal box to James. The pass
looked like it would sail over his head, but
James jumped. He headed the ball back
into the middle of the goal box.

A Bullfrog defender backed up to receive the ball, but Jax snuck in. He kicked the ball high and away to set up Marcus.

Marcus broke free and found his place. Flipping up and backward, Marcus tried a bicycle kick. His foot connected sharply with the ball, and it blasted into the goal.

"Goal!" shouted Jax. "Goal!"

James, Thomas, and Jax ran up to Marcus and helped him up from the ground in celebration. Marcus grinned down at Jax.

"I couldn't have done it without you, buddy," Marcus said.

"Well, you know what they say. Assists can be just as important as goals," said Jax. "Unless I'm the one scoring them," he added, joking.

"Like that will ever happen," said Marcus, laughing.

As he and his teammates celebrated, Jax knew he wouldn't be voted MVP of his team that season. But it didn't matter. *Winning as part of a team is way better than a stupid little trophy*, he thought.

ABOUT THE AUTHOR

Scott R. Welvaert lives in Chaska, Minnesota, with his wife and two daughters. He has written many children's books, including *The Curse of the Wendigo* and *The Mosquito King*. Most recently, he has written about Helen Keller, the Donner Party, and Thomas Edison. Scott enjoys playing video games and watching the Star Wars movies with his children.

ABOUT THE ILLUSTRATOR

When Sean Tiffany was growing up, he lived on a small island off the coast of Maine. Every day, from sixth grade until he graduated from high school, he had to take a boat to get to school. When Sean isn't working on his art, he works on a multimedia project called "OilCan Drive," which combines music and art. He has a pet cactus named Jim.

GLOSSARY

assists (uh-SISTS)—passes from a player to a teammate that make it possible to score a goal

commitment (kuh-MIT-ment)—a promise to do or support something

defender (de-FEN-dur)—a person playing defense, trying to keep the other team from scoring

fund-raising (FUHND-ray-zing)—activities done to raise money

intercepted (in-tur-SEPT-ed)—stole the ball

midfielder (MID-feel-dur)—part of the defense; they help with ball control and passing

position (puh-ZISH-uhn)—the role assigned to a player

striker (STRIKE-ur)—part of the offense; responsible for most of the scoring; also known as forward

transitions (tran-SISH-uhnz)—changes from one place to another

zone defense (ZOHN DI-fens)—a defensive plan where each player guards a certain area

DISCUSSION QUESTIONS

1. What are the pros and cons of Jax's decision to leave the Screaming Hawks and join the traveling team?

2. Coach wanted Jax to follow plays, while Jax just wanted to score. He argued that it didn't matter who got a goal since the score would be the same. Do you agree with Jax? Explain your answer.

3. Why did Coach Marcelo make Jax and Marcus work together for the fund-raiser?

WRITING PROMPTS

1. In this book, Jax learns about teamwork. Write a paragraph about what teamwork means to you.

2. Jax felt nervous at the traveling league soccer meeting. Write about a time that you felt nervous.

3. Write your own scene at a soccer game. Describe the action so that readers can picture it in their minds.

Traveling soccer teams are for players who are ready to take their game to the next level. In these programs, players compete against teams from other communities. Most players have a strong interest in soccer and are ready to devote more time to the sport. What can you expect from playing in traveling leagues?

WHO'S PLAYING: Kids as young as eight join traveling teams. These players have good ball handling skills. To compete, you need to be able to dribble, pass, and keep control of the ball with ease.

PRACTICE MAKES PERFECT: Teams typically practice two times a week for about an hour and a half each time. But that's not all — players are expected to practice on their own, too.

TRAVELING TEAM

GAME TIME: Games are normally on the weekends, with one or two games on either Saturday or Sunday.

MONEY TALK: Traveling teams are usually more expensive than recreation teams. This is to cover the costs of traveling, as well as tournament fees. Many teams hold fund-raising campaigns so that families are not required to pay for all the expenses themselves.

CAN YOU COMMIT? In addition to working hard during the season, you may be asked to attend soccer camps in the off season. In general, you'll have less time for other interests. Those who play on traveling teams feel the hard work is well worth it, though. It is exciting to play against other great players, and you're likely to become great friends with your fellow teammates.

3 MORE **GREAT BOOKS**